COMING HOME TO YOU

The day that you were born, my whole world came to life. You were so small and handsome, snuggled up in my arms. I wanted to stay there with you forever.

But then the call came, and I
had to leave, even though I
didn't want to. People needed
my help.

So, I held you close and kissed you goodbye for as long as I could. Then, I packed my gear and left for work.

I couldn't just leave you behind, so I put a picture of you in my pocket. I wanted to keep a piece of you with me wherever I went.

The first few days were busy as we hopped on an airplane and helicopter to fly across the world.

When we landed, I wasn't anywhere near you anymore, but I could feel you, like a magical string tied us together despite the miles.

Then, the days moved slower. I called you on the phone and watched every video our family sent.

I wrote you letters and smiled
every time I got one back.

I watched you grow with every month that passed and even though I hated being so far away from you, I loved seeing you hit every milestone.

And every day, I took your picture with me. I looked at it all the time. I looked at it when I was lonely

I looked at it when I was bored.

I looked at it when I was scared.

I looked at it when I was missing you.   I didn't like missing holidays and family dinners. I didn't like not being there to see your first smile in person, or hear your first laugh with my own ears.

I knew it wasn't forever. Then, after almost a year, it was time to come home.

I packed my bags, putting every letter and photo in a pocket to keep safe, and found myself on another airplane.

This time, with every mile we flew, I felt that magical string that connected us getting tighter…

This time, with every mile we flew, I felt that magical string that connected us getting tighter…

I got to see your face, hear your laugh and watch you crawl across our floor.

I got to feed you dinner and give you a bath.

And put you to bed for the first time in so long. I got to see all the ways you'd changed since I left and even though it hurt that I wasn't there to see it firsthand, I loved how much you'd grown.

As I sat there while you fell asleep, I pulled out that photo that I kept in my pocket the whole time I was gone and put it in my wallet. Even though you were right in front of me again, I wanted to keep you with me all the time.

I sat in the chair next to your bed, forever grateful to finally be home.

THE END